The Mag-spies

'The Mag-spies'
An original concept by Jenny Jinks
© Jenny Jinks

Illustrated by Kathryn Inkson

Published by MAVERICK ARTS PUBLISHING LTD
Studio 11, City Business Centre, 6 Brighton Road,
Horsham, West Sussex, RH13 5BB
© Maverick Arts Publishing Limited November 2020
+44 (0)1403 256941

A CIP catalogue record for this book is available at the British Library.

ISBN 978-1-84886-719-2

www.maverickbooks.co.uk

Gold

This book is rated as: Gold Band (Guided Reading)

The Mag-spies

By Jenny Jinks

Illustrated by
Kathryn Inkson

Chapter 1

Little Yawnton was just like any ordinary town. It had houses and a little village hall. In the middle of the village was a park, and in the middle of the park was a tall tree, where three magpies lived.

It might all seem very ordinary. However, Miles, Maggie and Max were no ordinary magpies.

They were the Mag-spies - highly trained spies, sent to watch over Little Yawnton and keep everyone safe.

You wouldn't know they were spies by looking at them, of course. That's because they were undercover.

Everything in Little Yawnton ran like clockwork. Every day was the same. At half past seven, Mr Grip fetched the milk bottles off his doorstep.

"It's Tuesday, must be porridge day," Maggie said. Sure enough, they saw Mr Grip through the window pouring the milk into a big bowl of porridge.

At quarter past ten, Mrs Banks walked round the park with her dog, Tibbles.

And in the evening, at half past eight, the street lamps went out and the residents of Little Yawnton went to bed.

Little Yawnton was so ordinary and boring, that sometimes the Mag-spies wondered why the chief had sent them there in the first place.

However, one perfectly normal Wednesday, something changed. Mrs Tibbs was late to her mid-morning yoga. Mrs Tibbs was never late. But that wasn't all.

She was late for her afternoon tea with Hilda too. Mrs Tibbs finally arrived to see Hilda standing at the door, huffing and tutting and checking her watch.

That's when Miles noticed it.

"Her watch! Mrs Tibbs's silver watch!" he said. "It's missing!"

"Are you sure?" said Maggie.

"Yes!" said Miles. "It's so shiny. I should have noticed it sooner!"

"It must have been stolen!" Max said. "Looks like the Mag-spies finally have a case."

Chapter 2

Max called an emergency meeting.

"Right," said Max, who had been elected as leader of the group (mainly because he had voted for himself). "If the thief has taken a watch, they might take something else as well. Miles, you keep a close eye on everyone else's valuables."

Miles flew off. He planned on taking his new role very seriously.

"Maggie, you go and look out for anyone acting suspiciously," Max said. "And I will keep tabs on Mrs Tibbs."

Maggie flapped away to sit on the highest branch of the tree where she had the best view over the town.

"Aaaaahhhhhh!" came an ear splitting screech later that day. "My gold necklace!"

"My gold rings!" came another cry.

"My gold watch!" shouted a third. There were cries and shouts from all over town.

"What is going on?" squawked Max.

"Now ALL the valuables in town have been stolen!" Maggie reported.

"From right under our beaks?" said Max. "This is serious. Very serious."

Chapter 3

Max called another emergency meeting (which was just Maggie and Max, because they couldn't find Miles).

"Did you see anything?" Max asked Maggie.

"No, nothing," said Maggie. "But I may have had my binoculars the wrong way round..."

She scratched her head, confused.

"We need to solve this before the chief finds out, or we'll all be fired!" Max said. "Have you seen Miles?"

"No, he must be very busy doing secret spy stuff," Maggie replied.

"Well we had better get back to keeping watch then," huffed Max.

Max flew around, keeping watch over the town all night. By the time the sun came up, he was exhausted. There was still no sign of the mystery thief. But luckily nothing else seemed to have been taken either.

Max flew sleepily back to HQ, ready for some much needed rest. Miles could take over the watch for a while, if anyone could find him.

But when Max got back, he suddenly didn't
feel like sleeping anymore.

"The missing gold!" he cried. "It's all here!"

Max swooped up to where Maggie had dozed off on her perch.

"Quick! Wake up! We're being framed!" said Max in a flap. "Someone has put all the missing jewellery in our headquarters! It's a set up!"

Maggie jumped awake. "What?!" she squawked. "But who would do such a thing?"

"Whoever it is, they must be real experts to have carried this off right under our beaks. We must work quickly. Have you seen Miles?"

Maggie shook her head.

"Well let's find him. And fast. Before things get any worse!"

Chapter 4

Maggie and Max flew all over town.

There was utter chaos down below. The residents of Little Yawnton were in uproar over the recent robberies. There were police everywhere. But there was still no sign of Miles.

"Maybe he's been stolen too?" suggested Maggie.

"Don't be ridiculous," said Max. "Stealing birds? Whoever heard of such a thing?" But even Max was starting to wonder.

Finally, they gave up and headed back to HQ. "Maybe we need to call the chief?" said Maggie. "I think we need back-up."

"And be caught red-winged with all the missing gold? First we need to get rid of the evidence. Quick, help me get it all out of here."

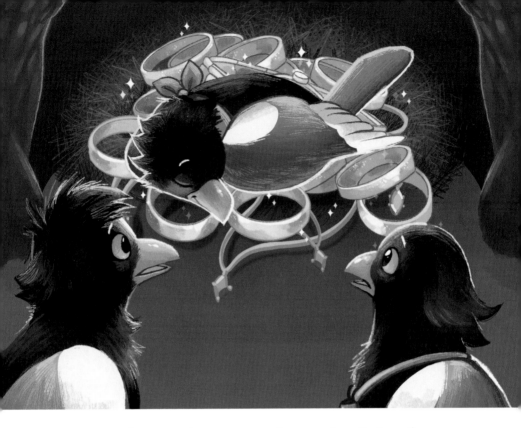

Max and Maggie scooped up wingfuls of jewellery. And there was Miles. He was fast asleep under the pile of gold.

"Miles!" shouted Max.

"Is it morning already? I just closed my eyes for a moment," Miles yawned.

"But... but what about all the gold?" Max said.

"Don't worry, it's all here." Miles said proudly.

"I know it is. The question is, why is it all here?"

"You said to keep a close eye on it, and where better to keep it all safe than right here in HQ," said Miles.

Max and Maddie opened and closed their beaks.

They were speechless!

"We have to put it all back," Max instructed.
"We can't get caught. We'll wait until
nightfall."

Max and Maggie flew out with the jewellery to put it all back (Miles had been given strict instructions to stay in HQ).

They didn't know where each thing belonged, but they hoped that nobody would notice.

They silently swooped into each house. But since the recent robberies, everyone had had burglar alarms installed.

Sirens blared. Lights flashed. Max and Maggie were surrounded.

"Scarper!" shouted Max. And they dropped everything and fled.

Chapter 5

"Well, that's that then. The mystery of the missing jewellery is solved," Maggie said the next day.

The Mag-spies were laying low in HQ so they wouldn't draw any attention to themselves, but feeling quite proud for solving the case... even if they were the ones who caused it.

"Yes. But there's something bothering me.

We still haven't found out what happened to Mrs Tibbs's silver watch," said Max. Just then, a van arrived at Mrs Tibbs's house.

"That's odd, it's not time for the milkman," Miles said. But it wasn't the milkman. A man delivered a package to Mrs Tibbs.

"Ah, my watch. I've been lost without it. It's so nice to have it fixed," she said, thanking the man.

The magpies looked at each other.
"I suppose life will go back to normal again now," Maggie sighed.

"I think I preferred it when it was boring and predictable," Miles said. "All that jewellery watching was far too stressful. I'm exhausted."

"I think we did pretty well though," Max said. "And to think, nobody ever suspected a thing."

The End

Book Bands for Guided Reading

The Institute of Education book banding system is a scale of colours that reflects the various levels of reading difficulty. The bands are assigned by taking into account the content, the language style, the layout and phonics. Word, phrase and sentence level work is also taken into consideration.

Maverick Early Readers are a bright, attractive range of books covering the pink to white bands. All of these books have been book banded for guided reading to the industry standard and edited by a leading educational consultant.

Pink
Red
Yellow
Blue
Green
Orange
Turquoise
Purple
Gold
White

To view the whole Maverick Readers scheme, visit our website at
www.maverickearlyreaders.com

Or scan the QR code above to view our scheme instantly!